for Luke, Sigrid, Karl, and Matthias Fostvedt

Distributed in the United States by Kodansha America, Inc., 114 Fifth
Avenue, New York New York 10011, and in the United Kingdom and
continental Europe by Kodansha Europe, Ltd.,
95 Aldwych, London WC2B 4JF.
Published by Kodansha International, Ltd., 17-14 Otowa 1-chome,
Bunkyo-ku, Tokyo 112, and Kodansha America, Inc.

Printed in Japan.
First edition, 1994
ISBN 4-7700-1850-9

94 95 96 10 9 8 7 6 5 4 3 2 1


Library of Congress Cataloging-in-Publication Data

McCarthy, Ralph F.
    Click-Clack Mountain / illustrations by Kokkan Otake : retold by
Ralph F. McCarthy.—1st ed.
        p.    cm.—(Kodansha children's classics series : 7)
    Summary: A thieving badger meets a dreadful fate.
    ISBN 4-7700-1850-9 :
    [1. Stories in rhyme. 2. Folklore—Japan.] I. Otake, Kokkan, ill.
II. Title.  III. Series
PZ8.3.M45936Cl 1994
398.21—dc20
(E)
                                                    94-626
                                                     CIP
                                                     AC

KODANSHA
CHILDREN'S CLASSICS

# CLICK-CLACK
# MOUNTAIN

Illustrations by Kokkan Odake
Retold by Ralph F. McCarthy

KODANSHA INTERNATIONAL
Tokyo • New York • London

Once upon a time in old Japan,
A farmer was out standing
      in his field.
"He grows the sweetest yams in all the land,"
      A hungry badger used to say
While watching from the
      woods each day
(But then again, to him
      *all* food appealed).

4

One night the badger
 came and made away
With all the yams his
 stubby arms could carry.
And when the farmer
 saw his field next day...

...He shook his fists and stamped his feet
And swore he'd trap and kill and *eat*
The thief. (You see, this man
was pretty scary.)

And, sure enough, one night the beast was caught:
The farmer found him struggling to get free.
"Aha!" the old man cried. "Just as I thought!
I've got you now, you little clown!"
He said, and hung him upside-down,
And took him home, and laughed with cruel glee.

The farmer told his
    rather foolish wife:
"Don't let this badger
    get the best of you!
While I'm out working,
    guard him with your life—
And when I'm back, we'll
    have some badger stew."

"Old woman!
    I've been
    such a
    hopeless
    sinner!"
The badger
    moaned.
    "And now
    I'll pay
    the price.
You've
    every
    right to
    cook me
    for your
    dinner...
But let me
    do just
    one good
    deed
Before
    I die—
    I see
    you need
Someone
    like me
    to help
    you pound
    your rice."

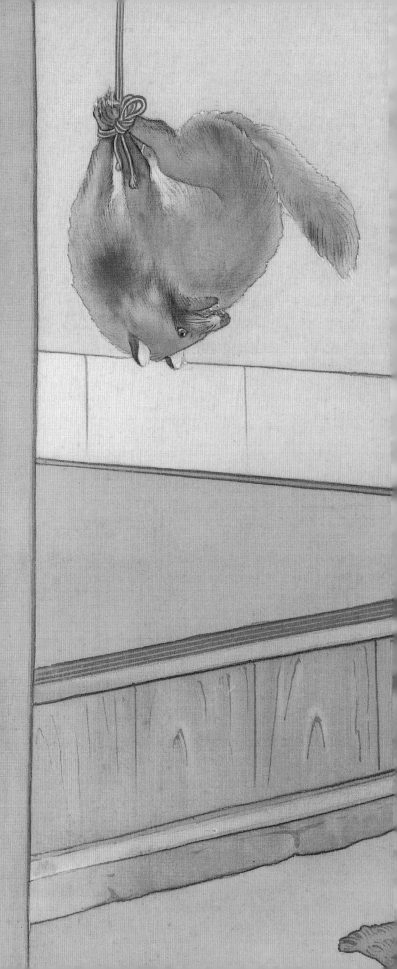

Now, as I said,
 this woman wasn't bright—
She let him down
 and handed him the pounder...

"All right,
then, *pound*!"
she said.
"I'll pound,
all right,"
The badger
laughed and
knocked her
down,
And left her
lying on
the ground,
And that
was how the
farmer later
found her.

This farmer had a
 rabbit for a friend
(In fact, it was the
 only friend he had),
Who listened to his
 story to the end,
And said:
 "That badger!
  *Boy*, he makes
  me mad!"

"Don't cry, old man—
   I'll make the rascal pay
For what he did to you,
   and to your wife.
Nobody ever liked him anyway—
No one would weep if *he*
   should lose his life!"

The next day, when the badger stepped outside,
He found the rabbit eating roasted beans.
"How good they smell! Please give me some!" he cried.
The rabbit said: "I *guess* I could,
If you'll just help me tote this wood..."
"Of course!" the badger squealed. "Oh, by all *means*!"

And once the wood was
    on the badger's back,
The rabbit took a flint
    and stone he'd found,
And struck the two together
    with a *clack*!
"What's that?" the
    badger said. "That
    *click-clack* sound?"

"Oh, that? It's nothing—
just the click-clack bird,
Who lives on Click-Clack Mountain
nowadays,"
The rabbit lied; another
*clack* was heard,
And sparks flew out
to set the wood
ablaze.

27

"What's that?" the badger
 stopped and said. "My word!
That crackling noise—
 it sounds like firewood burning!"

"It's nothing, badger, just
    the crackle-bird,
Who lives on Crackle Mountain. Say!
Let's go! I haven't got all day!
Just think of all
    the roasted beans
        you're earning!"

The stack of wood was really blazing now,
And soon the badger started to perspire.
He stopped to wipe the hot sweat off his brow...
Then suddenly began to cry:
"I'm burning up! Oh me! Oh my!"
And ran off screaming: "Help me! I'm on fire!"

And later, when the
  rabbit came to call,
He said: "Now, don't blame
  *me*—what could I do?
The sun was much too hot
  up there, that's all.
Don't worry, though—
  I've just the thing
To cure those burns…
  Now, this may sting,
But in a while you're
  sure to feel like new!"

The rabbit took some
  red-hot pepper paste,
And spread it up and down
  the badger's spine.
"It burns!" he cried. "My
  neck! My back! My waist!"
"Be brave!" the rabbit said.
  "You mustn't whine!"

The days went by—perhaps a week or two—
Before they met again, down by the sea.
"Hi, Rabbit...Yes, I'm better, thanks to you.
I've had enough of mountains, though—
It's way too hot up there, and so,
From here on in, the beach is where *I'll* be."

"You know," the rabbit said, "I've got a boat.
Why don't I make one more, from mud, for you,
So we can go out on the waves and float?"
"Oh, yes!" the badger said. "By all means, *do*!"

And when the boat was
    finished and in place,
The rabbit hopped aboard
    his own and said:

"You get the mud boat, badger. Come, let's race!
Just grab your oar and climb on in...
*Your* boat's brand new—I'm sure you'll win!"
And out into the wide, green sea they sped.

Of course, before they'd gotten far from shore,
The badger's boat began to fall apart.
"I'm sinking, rabbit! Quick, give me your oar!"
"*I'll* give it to you, pal—but this may smart!"

The rabbit dealt his foe a mighty blow,
And watched him as he sank beneath the foam.
And then, at sunset, in the crimson glow,
He calmly turned around and paddled home.

That night he told the farmer
what he'd done,
And both of them burst into
hearty laughter.
In old Japan, that's how
revenge was won...

But don't ask
what the
moral is—
I can't make
any promises
That *anyone*
was happy
ever after.

# KODANSHA CHILDREN'S CLASSICS

## THE ADVENTURES OF MOMOTARO, THE PEACH BOY
Illustrations by Ioe Saito
Retold by Ralph F. McCarthy

## THE MOON PRINCESS
Illustrations by Kancho Oda
Retold by Ralph F. McCarthy

## URASHIMA AND THE KINGDOM BENEATH THE SEA
Illustrations by Shiro Kasamatsu
Retold by Ralph F. McCarthy

## THE INCH-HIGH SAMURAI
Illustrations by Shiro Kasamatsu
Retold by Ralph F. McCarthy

## GRANDFATHER CHERRY-BLOSSOM
Illustrations by Eiho Hirezaki
Retold by Ralph F. McCarthy

## THE SPARROWS' INN
Illustrations by Choko Kamoshita
Retold by Ralph F. McCarthy

## CLICK-CLACK MOUNTAIN
Illustrations by Kokkan Odake
Retold by Ralph F. McCarthy

## THE MONKEY AND THE CRAB
Illustrations by Sengai Ikawa
Retold by Ralph F. McCarthy